Clara
the Chocolate
Fairy

Special thanks to Narinder Dhami

ISBN 978-0-545-60534-2

12 11 10 9 8 7 6 5 4 3 2 1   14 15 16 17 18 19/0

Printed in the U.S.A.   40

This edition first printing, March 2014

Clara
the Chocolate
Fairy

by Daisy Meadows

SCHOLASTIC INC.

The Fairyland Palace

Candy Land

Goblins' ice cream truck

Market booths

Charlie's ice cream truck

Kirsty's House

Wetherbury Village

I have a plan to make a mess
And cause the fairies much distress.
I'm going to take their charms away
And make my dreams come true today!

I'll build a castle made of sweets,
And ruin the fairies' silly treats.
I just don't care how much they whine,
Their cakes and candies will be mine!

Contents

Chocolate Crisis

"I'm so looking forward to this!" Rachel Walker told her best friend, Kirsty Tate, her voice brimming with excitement. The two girls were walking up one of the hills that overlooked Wetherbury. "I've never been to a candy factory before. I can't wait to see inside Candy Land."

"Me, neither," Kirsty agreed happily. "Wasn't it nice of Aunt Helen to arrange

a tour of the factory for my birthday?"
Kirsty's aunt worked in Candy Land's
cookie department.

"Yes, and your birthday isn't until
tomorrow, so it's
almost like having
an *extra* treat!"
Rachel pointed
out as they climbed
higher up the hill.
Ahead, they could
see the factory and

the big pink-and-white Candy Land sign
over the wrought-iron gates. "Do you
think we might get to try some treats
while we're on the tour?" Rachel asked
eagerly.

Kirsty grinned. "I hope so!" she
replied. "I'm really looking forward to

seeing the chocolate being made. My favorite kind is the Sticky Toffee Galore—it's a yummy toffee covered with chocolate!" Then Kirsty's smile faded. "Remember, though," she went on, "some of the treats might not taste very good, since Jack Frost and his goblins have the Sugar and Spice Fairies' magic charms."

Rachel nodded solemnly. Yesterday, right after she'd arrived to spend spring break with Kirsty, their old friend Honey the Candy Fairy had appeared to whisk the girls off to Fairyland. There they had met Honey's helpers—the seven Sugar and Spice Fairies! They looked after all the delicious, mouth-watering treats in Fairyland and the human world.

Rachel and Kirsty were very upset when they found out that Jack Frost and his goblins had stolen the Sugar and Spice Fairies' magic charms. But they couldn't believe it when they found out *why* Jack Frost needed the charms—he'd ordered his goblins to build him a castle made entirely of candy and treats!

To make things worse, King Oberon and Queen Titania had explained to the girls that Treat Day was coming up very soon. On Treat Day, the king and queen gave each fairy in Fairyland a basket full of yummy treats to thank them for their hard work all year. But this year there wouldn't be any treat baskets at all if the magic charms weren't returned to the Sugar and Spice Fairies. Jack Frost had given the seven charms to his goblins to protect in the human world. Rachel and Kirsty had promised to help their fairy friends find them. Then treats everywhere would taste delicious again, and Treat Day wouldn't be ruined for all the fairies.

"It's not just my birthday tomorrow," Kirsty said. "It's Treat Day in Fairyland, too! We *have to* find the missing magic charms before then, Rachel."

Rachel nodded. "Three down, four to go!" she said with a smile. "We're going to find them all, Kirsty—I just know it!"

"I wonder if we'll see one of our fairy friends at Candy Land today?" Kirsty remarked. "Maybe Jack Frost and his goblins will be there, too."

"We'll be ready for them!" Rachel replied. "Look, isn't that Aunt Helen waiting for us under the Candy Land sign?"

Aunt Helen waved as Rachel and Kirsty hurried toward the factory gates.

"You're right on time, girls," she said with a smile. "Come with me! I'll take you to the reception area where the rest of the tour group is waiting. Are you looking forward to seeing the factory?"

"Oh, YES!" Kirsty and Rachel cried together. Aunt Helen laughed. She led the girls through the gates to a door with RECEPTION printed on it. Inside the office

were several people waiting for the tour,
including an older couple and some
families with young kids.

The first thing Kirsty noticed in the
reception area was the wonderful, sweet,
sugary smell! She breathed in deeply, and
then smiled when she saw Rachel doing
exactly the same thing.

"Girls, I have to rush back to the cookie department," Aunt Helen told them. "One of the guides, Matt, will show you around, and I'll meet you in the cafeteria later for lunch."

"Thanks, Aunt Helen," Kirsty replied.

A few minutes after Aunt Helen left, a tall man wearing a white apron and hat bounded into the office.

"Welcome to Candy Land!" he announced, beaming at everyone. "I'm Matt, your tour guide today. I'm going to explain how our fabulous, mouthwatering treats are made, and you'll get to try some of them, too."

The girls exchanged delighted glances. Yum!

"This way to the tasting room!" Matt announced, opening a door on the other side of the office. Everyone filed into a bright room that had walls painted with pink-and-white stripes. On a table in the middle of the room were sparkly pink-and-white gift boxes filled with delicious-looking chocolates.

"Look, Sticky Toffee Galore!" Rachel murmured, pointing out one of the boxes to Kirsty.

"Please help yourselves," Matt told them. "Then we'll go into the factory, and you can see exactly how your favorite chocolates are made."

Everyone gathered around the table. Kirsty selected a Sticky Toffee Galore and eagerly popped it into her mouth. But the bitterness of the chocolate made her  gasp in disgust. It tasted *terrible*!

Rachel had chosen Golden Crunch, a star-shaped chocolate filled with honeycomb. But, like Kirsty, she was also in for a shock when she tasted it.

"This is awful!" Rachel muttered to Kirsty, trying to swallow the bitter chocolate as fast as possible. "It's the worst chocolate I've ever had!"

Kirsty glanced around the tasting room. The other tour members were looking unimpressed with the chocolates, too. The older couple was making faces at the taste, and one of the little kids burst into tears.

"Gross chocolate, Mommy!" she wailed.

Matt looked flustered. "Oh, I don't know what's wrong today!" he said apologetically. "The chocolate tasting is usually a highlight of the tour. Let's move on."

"This is all because Jack Frost and his goblins have the Sugar and Spice Fairies' charms!" Rachel whispered.

Kirsty nodded in agreement as Matt ushered them out of the tasting room.

"So, here we are in the Candy Land factory," Matt announced. Everyone looked around with interest. The sugary smell was even stronger now, and Rachel and Kirsty could see lots of shiny silver machines making different treats and chocolates. They were operated by workers in spotless white aprons and hats like Matt's.

"This is where the chocolates are packaged," Matt went on. He led the group over to a conveyor belt full of chocolates wrapped in brightly colored foil. A young woman was carefully packing them into gift boxes. "Meet Suzy," Matt said with a grin. "She's the fastest packer in the factory!"

"Hello, everyone." Suzy smiled as she popped the last chocolate into the gift box she was holding, closed it, and set it aside. She immediately began filling an empty box, without letting a single chocolate on the conveyor belt get past her!

"See what I mean?" Matt said, and everyone laughed.

"The foil wrappers look pretty, but the chocolates will taste horrible, thanks to Jack Frost!" Kirsty murmured to Rachel.

Rachel was about to reply when one of the wrappers moving toward them on the conveyor belt caught her eye.

The wrapper was surrounded by a faint golden glow. As Rachel looked more closely, her heart skipped a beat.

"Kirsty, that's not a chocolate wrapper!" she whispered, pointing at the conveyor belt excitedly. "It's Clara the Chocolate Fairy!"

Storeroom
Surprise

Surprised, Kirsty peered at the conveyor belt and saw the tiny fairy, wearing a pretty purple dress and cropped silver leggings. Clara was waving frantically at them.

"Clara's getting closer to where Suzy's packing the gift boxes!" Kirsty said with a worried frown. "If she flies away now, Suzy will see her—"

"And if she stays on the conveyor belt, Clara will end up in a box of chocolates!" Rachel added. "Oh, Kirsty, we have to help her."

"I'll try to distract Suzy," Kirsty decided. The rest of the group was gathered around, watching Suzy pack the chocolates. Kirsty hurried to join them.

"Could you tell us what all the different flavors are, Suzy?" Kirsty asked.

"Yes, of course," Suzy replied. She turned away from the conveyor belt to glance at Kirsty.

"We have raspberry ripple, strawberry and vanilla cream, caramel, peanut—" Clara fluttered up from the conveyor belt while Suzy wasn't looking, her long blonde hair streaming behind her. She slipped inside Rachel's bag.

"Thank you, girls," Clara gushed when Kirsty rejoined them. "I thought I was going to be packed inside a gift box! I'm here because Jack Frost and his goblins are somewhere in Candy Land—and they have my cocoa bean charm!"

"Come on, you two," Matt called to Rachel and Kirsty as the rest of the tour group moved on. "We're going to look at a giant vat of liquid chocolate!"

"We'll try our best to get your charm back, Clara," Kirsty promised. "Chocolate really tastes horrible without it!"

Matt and the rest of the group were already gathered around the huge vat of swirling milk chocolate. Clara ducked out of sight as Kirsty and Rachel went to join them.

"When the chocolate is liquid like this, it can be poured into different-shaped molds to set," Matt was explaining. "And then—"

Before Matt could finish, the chocolate suddenly began to flow over the sides of the vat! It splashed all over the floor, just missing Matt's shoes.

"Oh, no!" Matt exclaimed, waving for the tour group to move back. "I don't know why everything's going wrong today!" He jumped aside as more chocolate spilled onto the floor.

"Could someone help fix this, please?" Matt called across the room to some other employees. Then he turned back to the tour group. "Let's go, and I'll show you our chocolate molds."

Matt escorted the group across the

factory to look at the molds. There were lots of different shapes—hearts, stars, diamonds, and eggs—but Rachel and Kirsty could see that the molds were all cracked and bent out of shape.

"I'm so sorry, everyone," Matt muttered, looking very embarrassed.

"Poor Matt," Clara whispered to the girls as the guide quickly led them away again. "This isn't his fault—it's all because Jack Frost has my cocoa bean charm!"

Kirsty glanced around curiously as Matt took them to another corner of the factory. There, she saw a huge silver machine squirting chocolate on rows and rows of sticky toffee bars.

"The machine is making Sticky Toffee Galores!" Kirsty exclaimed, thrilled.

"That's right," Matt said. "And everything seems to be running smoothly here, thank goodness!"

Next to the machine, Rachel noticed a factory worker. He was wearing the same white apron and hat as the others, and he was eating a Sticky Toffee Galore very enthusiastically.

"It looks like this batch of chocolates tastes okay," Rachel said quietly to

Kirsty. "Not like the one you had!"

Matt was frowning at the worker. "You know you shouldn't be eating on the factory floor!" he scolded. "It's against the rules."

"I'm a new taste tester," the worker mumbled through a mouthful of chocolate and toffee, turning away.

As Matt began telling the group about the machine, Rachel watched the worker hurry over to a cart piled with chocolate. He rushed off with the trolley, but he was going much too fast. Suddenly, he tripped on the hem of his long apron and

went head over heels! Rachel gasped as
she saw a pair of big green feet sticking
out from beneath the apron.

"That worker's a goblin!" Rachel
whispered excitedly to Kirsty and Clara.

"Then we have no time to waste!"
declared Clara. "He must have my
cocoa bean charm. Quickly, girls!
Let me turn you into fairies before we
lose him."

Their hearts pounding, Kirsty and
Rachel slipped out of sight behind the big
silver machine. A cloud of dazzling
sparkles from
Clara's wand
shrank the girls
down to
fairy-size!
Fluttering their
wings, the three
friends zoomed
up into the air.

"There he goes!"
Kirsty said, pointing at the goblin racing
across the factory with the cart.

"Stay up high so that no one spots us,
girls," Clara warned them.

Rachel, Kirsty, and Clara darted
across the factory, keeping the goblin in

sight. They saw him hurry down a
hallway, pushing the cart ahead of him,
and stop by a large metal door marked
STOREROOM.

Clara and the girls watched as the
goblin yanked the door open.

"He's going inside," Rachel whispered.
"We have to follow him," said Clara
urgently.

The goblin shoved his cart through the open door and then let it close behind him. Rachel, Kirsty, and Clara managed to fly through just before the door banged shut. They perched on the door frame and looked around the storeroom.

What an extraordinary sight! The storeroom was filled with all kinds of chocolates. There were piles of foil-wrapped chocolates on the floor, and empty boxes tossed into a corner. There

were chocolates in different shapes—
hearts, stars, and lots of others—and
stacks of chocolate bars, too.

And in the middle of the room, sitting
on a heap of Sticky Toffee Galore and
giggling with glee, was Jack Frost
himself!

At the Candy Castle

"Give me the magic cocoa bean charm!"
Jack Frost demanded, glaring at the
goblin with the cart.

Clara glanced at Rachel and Kirsty in
dismay as Jack Frost snatched the charm
from the goblin. Jack Frost hung it
around his neck and held the charm up,
so that it caught the light and sparkled
with magic.

"How are we going to get my charm back *now*?" Clara whispered, biting her lip anxiously. She looked so worried that Kirsty and Rachel knew they had to do something. Glancing at each other, they swooped down together toward Jack Frost.

"Fairies!" yelled the goblin, pointing at them. Jack Frost scowled, hiding the cocoa bean charm around his neck with one icy hand.

"What do *you* want?" he sneered.

"You know, you have lots of chocolate here, and it's greedy to keep it for yourself," Kirsty began. "You're causing trouble at Candy Land, too!"

"Clara needs her magic charm so that things can get back to normal," added Rachel.

Jack Frost cackled loudly. "I don't care about Candy Land, and I don't care about silly fairies!" he said. "I need tons of chocolate for my Candy Castle!" He waved his wand to conjure a bolt of icy magic. Instantly, Jack Frost, his goblin, and all the chocolate in the storeroom vanished. Clara and the girls were alone in an empty room.

"They've taken all the chocolate to the Candy Castle!" Clara gasped. "Let's go, girls!"

This time, it was Clara who waved her wand. Her fairy magic whisked all three of them off to Fairyland! A few moments later, they were fluttering above the chocolate wafer drawbridge in front of Jack Frost's Candy Castle. Luckily, they were small enough that the goblins couldn't spot them from the ground!

"The castle's getting bigger!" Rachel exclaimed. "That's why Jack Frost needs more and more treats."

Kirsty frowned. "See those holes in the cookie walls?" she asked. "Some of the colorful gumdrop decorations are missing, too."

Clara was looking around the castle gardens. "The chocolate statue of Jack Frost only has one hand, and some of Lisa the Lollipop Fairy's lollipop flowers are missing!" she announced. "Only the lollipop sticks are left in the ground."

Clara, Rachel, and Kirsty flew along the drawbridge to the enormous chocolate door that led into the castle. Jack Frost stood in front of the door, yelling at a group of goblin builders. As Clara and the girls got closer, they could see that a big bite had been taken right out of the middle of the door!

"You fools!" Jack Frost shouted furiously. "You're supposed to be *building* my castle, not *eating* it!"

Clara, Rachel, and Kirsty glanced at one another. They couldn't help smiling. They all knew how greedy the goblins could be!

"No more snacking on my sweet treats!" Jack Frost ordered, fixing the goblins with a cold stare. "I want my castle finished *immediately*!"

As Jack Frost continued to yell, Kirsty noticed a goblin crouching in the shadow of the chocolate door. She could see that he was chewing on the strawberry laces that held up the chocolate wafer drawbridge. Kirsty nudged Rachel and Clara to warn them, and the three of them fluttered safely up into the air. Just

then, Jack Frost spotted them and shook
his fist.

"Pesky fairies!" he roared. "You'll *never*
get the magic cocoa bean charm away
from me!" As the drawbridge crashed
into the milkshake moat with a loud
splash, Jack Frost dashed inside the
Candy Castle.

Tile Trouble

"Come on, girls!" Clara cried. Without
a second to waste, she, Rachel, and
Kirsty flew into the castle after Jack
Frost. He began dodging in and out of
different rooms, trying to get away, but
Clara and the girls could always hear
him yelling at the greedy goblins as he
ran by.

"Stop eating my dining room!" Jack
Frost shouted at some goblins munching
on a table and chairs made from mint-
chocolate wafers. Clara, Rachel, and
Kirsty flew close behind as he rushed
through the Great Hall, where a goblin
was nibbling at a picture frame made of
golden honeycomb.

"Soon there will be no Candy Castle
left!" Jack Frost wailed. He gave a yelp
of rage as he ran past another room.
"Don't eat my ice cream!" he shouted.
Kirsty peeked into the bathroom as she,
Clara, and Rachel flew by. She could
see a goblin gobbling scoops of Esme
the Ice Cream Fairy's green ice cream
from the tub.

Jack Frost dashed up the winding staircase, where a goblin was munching on the cookie steps. Then he turned down a chocolate-paneled hallway. Clara, Rachel, and Kirsty zoomed after him and saw that the hallway was a dead end.

"We've got him cornered, girls!" Clara sighed with relief.

But Jack Frost cackled at them and pressed a white chocolate button on one of the panels. A secret door slid open and Jack Frost smiled smugly.

"Good–bye, foolish fairies!" he shouted. He rushed through the door, but instead of closing it behind him, Jack Frost stopped short and let out a shriek of horror. "Oh, no! My candy bedroom is ruined!" he wailed. *"Ruined!"*

Clara, Rachel, and Kirsty flew into the room behind him. An enormous bed made of soft marshmallow had big bites taken out of it. The dark chocolate furniture had some drawers and doorknobs missing. On the nightstand, Rachel saw the throne decoration from Coco the Cupcake Fairy, but all that was left of the cupcake it had been on were a few crumbs.

Jack Frost gazed at the floor, sniffling.

Why is he so upset about the floor? Kirsty wondered, staring down at it. The floor was covered with tiles of white, milk, and dark chocolate, but some of them had obviously been nibbled away. Kirsty peered at it more closely— 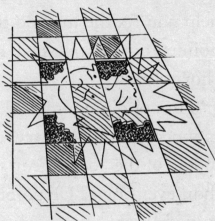 and finally realized that the floor had been a tile portrait of Jack Frost. Now some of the tiles had been gobbled up by the goblins, including Jack Frost's nose! Kirsty pointed this out to Clara and Rachel as Jack Frost sobbed.

"My beautiful floor!" he groaned, icy tears dripping down his face. "It was a wonderful work of chocolate art."

Rachel fluttered forward. "Clara can help you fix the missing tiles," she pointed out, "*if* you give her magic charm back."

"I'm not giving it back!" Jack Frost snapped. "Can't you see? I need the magic of the cocoa bean charm more than ever now!" He pointed at the ruined floor.

Kirsty stared down at the chocolate tiles. Suddenly, her own favorite chocolate, the Sticky Toffee Galore, popped into her head. That gave her an idea!

A Sticky Situation!

Kirsty turned to Clara and Rachel and whispered her plan.

Clara smiled. "I know a fairy who can help you," she told Jack Frost.

The girls watched as Clara waved her wand, writing a glittering word in the air—*Lizzie*. A second later, Lizzie the Sweet Treats Fairy appeared in a cloud of magical sparkles.

"Hello, everyone!" Lizzie cried.

"Hello, Lizzie," Kirsty and Rachel said together, beaming at their old friend. Lizzie was one of the Princess Fairies.

Jack Frost groaned loudly. "More fairies!" he muttered. "Go away and leave me alone!"

"Lizzie's going to make your chocolate tile floor even better than it was before," Rachel told him. She murmured something quietly to Lizzie, who smiled and nodded.

"Hurry up, then!" Jack Frost said rudely.

Lizzie waved her wand. Sparkling fairy dust flew to the four corners of the room, floating softly down onto the ruined tiles. In a flash, the missing tiles were replaced. The floor looked as good as new, complete with a tile picture of Jack Frost's face!

"Hooray!" Jack Frost cried excitedly. "My chocolate floor is perfect again!

Don't I look handsome?" He proudly tried to rush forward to get a better look at his giant portrait, but his feet wouldn't move. Rachel and Kirsty grinned at each other.

"What's going on?" Jack Frost roared. "I'm stuck! My feet are stuck to the floor!" He bent over and stared at the tiles more closely. Then he gave another scream of rage. "These tiles aren't chocolate— they're *toffee*!"

Furious, Jack Frost swatted at the four fairies hovering above him, but they flew out of his reach.

Jack Frost tried to stamp his feet in a rage, but he couldn't — he was completely stuck to the toffee! Rachel fluttered over to him. Dodging his flailing arms, she managed to unhook the cocoa bean charm from his necklace.

"I think this belongs to someone else," Rachel said, shaking her head.

"Give it back!" Jack Frost demanded, but Rachel ignored him and flew over to

Clara. Clara beamed when Rachel
handed her the glowing charm. It
became fairy-sized
the instant Clara
touched it.

"Thank
you, girls!
And thank
you, Lizzie,
for all your
help!" Clara
declared, clasping
the magic cocoa
bean tightly. "Now
Lizzie and I need to
return to Fairyland and share the good
news with everyone."

"But we can't leave Jack Frost stuck in
the toffee!" Kirsty pointed out.

"Oops, I almost forgot!" Clara giggled. With a flick of her wand, the toffee tiles turned back into chocolate. Jack Frost stopped yelling and looked thrilled, instead.

"My beautiful floor is back!" he exclaimed, dancing around with glee. "And the chocolate me looks marvelous!"

Rachel, Kirsty, Clara, and Lizzie laughed.

"But that's *all* the chocolate you're getting!" Kirsty warned Jack Frost as he continued to dance happily around the room. Then, a flick of Clara's wand whisked Rachel and Kirsty back to Candy Land.

Chocolate Is Magical!

Before long, the girls were back in the Candy Land factory again, and at their normal human size. They hurried out from behind the Sticky Toffee Galore machine to join the rest of the group. Kirsty was relieved that no one seemed to have noticed they were missing.

"And now you're going to see where we keep our chocolate before they're sent out to the candy stores," Matt was saying. "Follow me, everyone."

Matt led the way across the factory floor and down a hallway. The girls exchanged anxious glances.

"This is the way we chased the goblin with the cart," Rachel whispered to Kirsty. "Matt's taking us to the storeroom."

"But we know the storeroom's empty!" Kirsty said, looking very worried. "Jack Frost took all the chocolate for his Candy Castle. What's

Matt going to say when he sees there's nothing there?"

"Here we are." Matt stopped outside the door marked STOREROOM. The girls held their breath as he pushed the door open.

To Rachel and Kirsty's delight, they could see that the room was full of chocolate again! But this time, the gift boxes were arranged in neat piles, the chocolate bars were stacked nicely, and there were no heaps of chocolate on the floor.

"Clara must have used her magic to return it all," Rachel whispered happily. "And she cleaned up the mess Jack Frost and his goblin made, too."

"Look, she even left us some more samples to try!" Kirsty said, pointing to a tray of chocolate sitting on a table.

Matt was checking out the samples, looking surprised. "Well, we usually put out all our samples in the tasting room," he said with a smile. "But let's try these, too."

Kirsty chose another Sticky Toffee Galore, and so did Rachel. This time, the chocolates tasted delicious.

"*Mmm!*" was all Rachel could say for a moment as she enjoyed the combination of delicious chocolate and sticky toffee. The rest of the tour group was also *ooh*ing and *aah*ing as they ate their samples. Even

Matt picked a Sticky Toffee Galore and popped it in his mouth.

"Magical!" he said.

Rachel and Kirsty grinned at each other.

Rachel laughed. "That's exactly what I think, too!" she said.

After the tour, the girls thanked Matt
and then hurried to meet Aunt Helen in
the cafeteria. She was sitting at a table,
waiting for them.

"I hope you
had a good
time, girls,"
Aunt Helen
said with
a smile.
"And I hope
you're not
too sick of
chocolate, because
there's chocolate cake for dessert!"

"Yum!" Kirsty said. "We'd never get
sick of chocolate, would we, Rachel?"

"No way!" Rachel agreed. "And we're
having a great time."

"Well, I hope you'll have fun this afternoon with me in the cookie department, too," Aunt Helen said. "Now, let's go and order our lunch."

Rachel and Kirsty glanced meaningfully at each other as they followed Aunt Helen to the cafeteria counter. Treat Day was getting closer and closer! They'd returned four of the Sugar and Spice Fairies' magic charms, but there were still three left to find. Could they get them back before

64

Treat Day was ruined for everyone in Fairyland? Or would they run out of time? One thing was for sure—they were in for a lot more magical adventures!

Rachel and Kirsty found Lisa, Esme, Coco,
and Clara's missing magic charms.
Now it's time for them to help

Madeline
the Cookie Fairy!

Join their next adventure in this
special sneak peek. . . .

In the Candy Land Cafeteria

The yellow walls of the Candy Land factory were gleaming in the midday sun, and the colorful flags on its roof waved in the spring breeze. In the factory cafeteria, Rachel Walker and Kirsty Tate were finishing their sandwiches and chatting with Kirsty's aunt Helen.

"You're so lucky to work here," Rachel said. "It's my dream job!"

"You wouldn't say that if you saw all the paperwork I have to do," replied Aunt Helen with a laugh.

"Yes, but you get to taste all the new candy," said Kirsty with a giggle. "That sounds like the best job in the world!"

Aunt Helen laughed and glanced up at the clock on the wall.

"It *does* mean I was able to organize a tour of the factory for my favorite niece and her best friend!" she said with a smile. "Have you enjoyed the tour so far?"

Tomorrow was Kirsty's birthday, and this special day at Candy Land was an early birthday treat. Since Rachel was staying with Kirsty over spring break, she had gotten to come along. Lucky her!

"It's been amazing!" said Rachel. "The chocolate department was really cool."

"Yes, thank you for the tickets, Aunt Helen," said Kirsty. "Today is one of the best birthday presents I've ever had!"

"It's not over yet," said Aunt Helen with a grin. "You'll be spending this afternoon with me in the cookie department. But first, I have another little treat for you. Wait here! I'll be right back."

She winked at them and headed up to the cafeteria counter. Rachel and Kirsty looked at each other with shining eyes.

"I don't know how this day could get any better!" said Rachel. "Isn't this just perfect?"

She waved her arm around at the

cafeteria tables and chairs. Everything at
Candy Land was made to look like sweet
treats, so the tables were huge cakes and
the chairs were enormous cookies.

"Look," whispered Kirsty, nudging her
best friend. "That boy's got a Sticky
Toffee Galore. They're my favorite."

RAINBOW magic™

Which Magical Fairies Have You Met?

- ☐ The Rainbow Fairies
- ☐ The Weather Fairies
- ☐ The Jewel Fairies
- ☐ The Pet Fairies
- ☐ The Dance Fairies
- ☐ The Music Fairies
- ☐ The Sports Fairies
- ☐ The Party Fairies
- ☐ The Ocean Fairies
- ☐ The Night Fairies
- ☐ The Magical Animal Fairies
- ☐ The Princess Fairies
- ☐ The Superstar Fairies
- ☐ The Fashion Fairies
- ☐ The Sugar & Spice Fairies

SCHOLASTIC

HiT entertainment

Find all of your favorite fairy friends at
scholastic.com/rainbowmagic

RMFAIRY9

RAINBOW magic™

SPECIAL EDITION

Which Magical Fairies Have You Met?

3 stories in each one!

- ☐ Joy the Summer Vacation Fairy
- ☐ Holly the Christmas Fairy
- ☐ Kylie the Carnival Fairy
- ☐ Stella the Star Fairy
- ☐ Shannon the Ocean Fairy
- ☐ Trixie the Halloween Fairy
- ☐ Gabriella the Snow Kingdom Fairy
- ☐ Juliet the Valentine Fairy
- ☐ Mia the Bridesmaid Fairy
- ☐ Flora the Dress-Up Fairy
- ☐ Paige the Christmas Play Fairy
- ☐ Emma the Easter Fairy
- ☐ Cara the Camp Fairy
- ☐ Destiny the Rock Star Fairy
- ☐ Belle the Birthday Fairy
- ☐ Olympia the Games Fairy
- ☐ Selena the Sleepover Fairy
- ☐ Cheryl the Christmas Tree Fairy
- ☐ Florence the Friendship Fairy
- ☐ Lindsay the Luck Fairy
- ☐ Brianna the Tooth Fairy
- ☐ Autumn the Falling Leaves Fairy
- ☐ Keira the Movie Star Fairy
- ☐ Addison the April Fool's Day Fairy

■ SCHOLASTIC

Find all of your favorite fairy friends at
scholastic.com/rainbowmagic

HIT entertainment

RMSPECIAL12